© Éditions Philippe Auzou, 2009
First published in France by éditions Auzou, 2009
Original title: À la recherche du bonheur

Published in the United States and its territories by
HAMMOND WORLD ATLAS CORPORATION
Part of the Langenscheidt Publishing Group
36-36 33rd Street
Long Island City, NY 11106

Translator : Andrew Weller

Printed and bound in China

ISBN-13: 978-0841-671416

In Search of
Happiness

By Juliette Saumande

Illustrations by Eric Puybaret

The people who lived in Prudence were very lucky: not a single one of them was unhappy!

They never baked cakes (for fear of making a mess),

They never played with their toys (for fear of breaking them),

They never went on trips (for fear of getting lost).

Since they never took chances, they were never disappointed.

Hundreds of curious folk came from all over the world to discover their secret!

But . . .

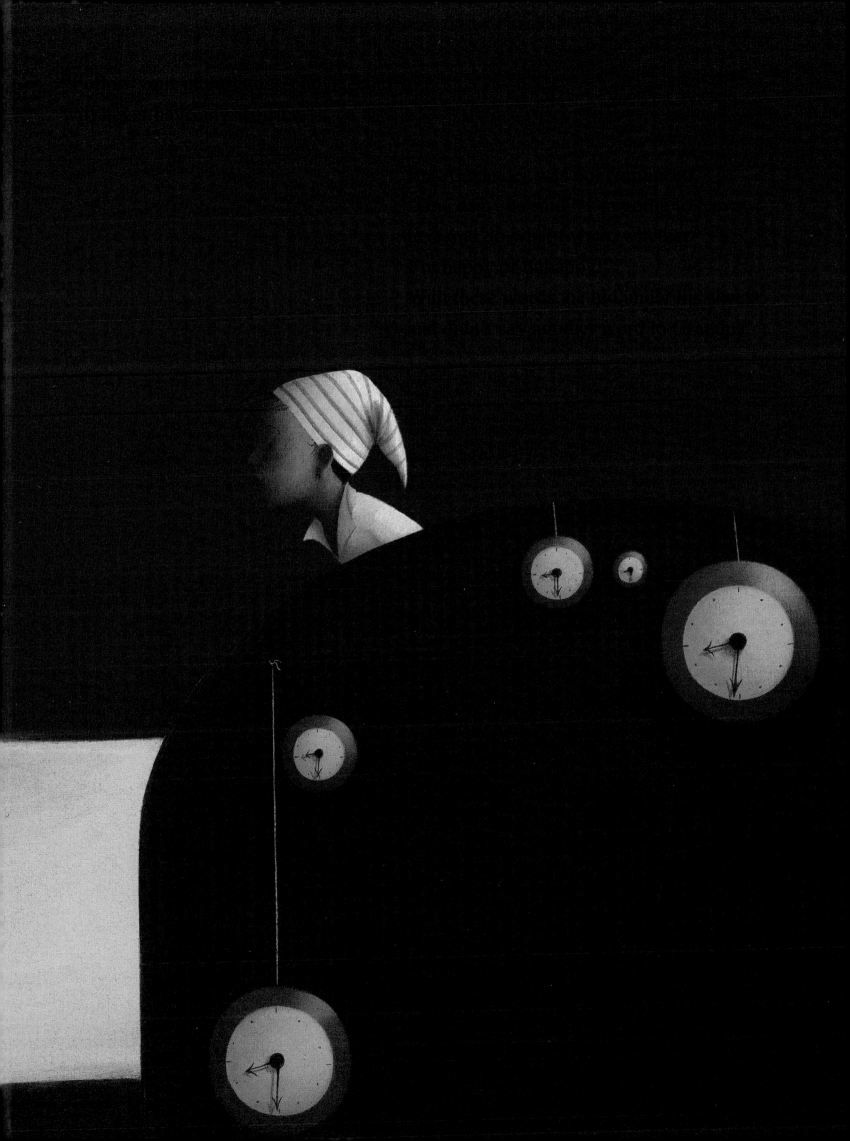

Alexander was still sulking in his bed when, suddenly,
the window opened, and a songbird landed in front of him.

"I am Paradiso," the bird said.

"The Night Wind whispered in my ear and told me that you wanted to go away. I am going to the Land of Happiness. Do you want to come with me?"

Alexander walked for a long time. At dawn, he reached
a beach with white sand. There, he found a tiny boat.
He jumped in and rowed with all his might.

But soon a storm came. . .

. . . and the small boat tossed, and turned, and flipped over.

Alexander thrashed about in the sea
with his arms and feet, swallowing
big mouthfuls of salty water.

When the sea finally spit him out again,
he was completely discouraged.
"It's hopeless! Paradiso has disappeared,
and here I am, all alone in a strange land!"
He sat down on the pebbles and began to cry.

The little castaway, starving, set off once again.

He arrived at a village and asked for something to eat.

"Pick some fruit," the villagers told him.

"But what if it's not ripe?" Alexander asked.

"Or if it's too ripe?"

"It's worth trying," said one man,

"Because our trees grow candy!"

Alexander could not resist. The first piece of candy he picked was as hard as a rock, and the second was total mush and trickled between his teeth. But the third . . . the third was absolutely delicious!

That evening, Alexander wrote

his first postcard.

"Dear Grandpa,
I'm here in the Land of Happiness! People eat sweets all day
long (good ones and bad ones!). My teeth are hurting a bit,
but other than that, it's amazing!
Lots of love,
Alexander."

At that very moment, Paradiso appeared.
"So, how do you like the Isle of Treats?" he said.
"What? This isn't the Land of Happiness?"
"It's here . . ." the bird replied, "and elsewhere.
But I must be going soon. Do you want to come with me tomorrow?"

The next day, Alexander was curious, so he decided to continue on.
He would find the Land of Happiness no matter what!
He set off in the same direction as his winged friend
and came to the land of a great wizard.
"Ask me for whatever you want," the wizard said to him,
"and it will be yours."
Alexander was wary.
"But what if I don't like it?" he asked.
"Then you'll just have to make another choice!"

Alexander asked for . . . a talking rabbit, dinosaur teeth, a fancy racing car,
and a wand for seeking gold. He received all that he asked for.

"Unbelievable! Here, it's Christmas everyday!"

That evening, Alexander wrote another postcard to Grandpa telling him about everything that had happened.

"It's too bad you're not here to see it.
I can't take anything with me because it all disappears once you leave the wizard's land. So I have decided to stay!"

He had just added "Lots of love," when Paradiso arrived.
"This time, I am here!" Alexander declared.
"In the Land of Happiness!"
"Yes and no," replied the bird.
"This is the Gorge of the Spoiled Ones."
The beautiful bird spread its wings and flew away.

Alexander couldn't get over it.
"Could I be even happier somewhere else?"
He definitely wanted to see that!

The following day, Alexander climbed to the top of a mountain.
There, some little girls were having a snowball fight.
"Do you want to play?" they asked.
Alexander thought about it, "Grandpa would tell me,
'You might catch a cold.'"
But Grandpa wasn't there, and Alexander said, "Yes."
Later, he wrote to Grandpa:

"I've got bruises everywhere, but I had so much fun!
This must be the Land of Happy People!"

And yet Paradiso
told him once again,
"You are both right and wrong.
This is the Glacier of the Frozen Ones."

So Alexander went down the mountain
where he met an old lady, who said to him,
"You look like a nice boy
and you walk like a real mountaineer.
Come to the castle, and I will introduce you
to everyone."

Alexander was in heaven.

At the castle, he received so many compliments
that his cheeks turned bright red.
That evening, he sent kisses to Grandpa.
"Now you are in the Valley of the Delighted," said Paradiso.
"As for me, I'm going on. Do you want to come with me?"
"Compliments are very nice," Alexander thought.
"But I'm afraid I'll get bored here."
So he replied:
"Yes, yes, and three times yes!"

Meanwhile, Grandpa read and reread Alexander's postcards. If he had the courage, he would have joined his grandson right away.

After all, he too would have liked to visit the Land of the Sweetie Pies where mothers never have cold hands and cuddle with their little ones all the time. And the Town of Good Friends or the Bay of the Beautiful Music seemed really amazing too!

But Grandpa didn't go.
Oh, how he sometimes regretted being so careful!

Alexander had traveled
for almost a year.
In each new country, he thought:
"I've found it!"
But Paradiso would always
tell him:

"It's true . . . and it's not true."

The little traveler wondered if the country
he was searching for really existed.
But the journey was so much fun!
More and more often, though, he thought
about Grandpa, so far away, and he began
to see that reaching the Land of Happiness
might not be the most important thing.

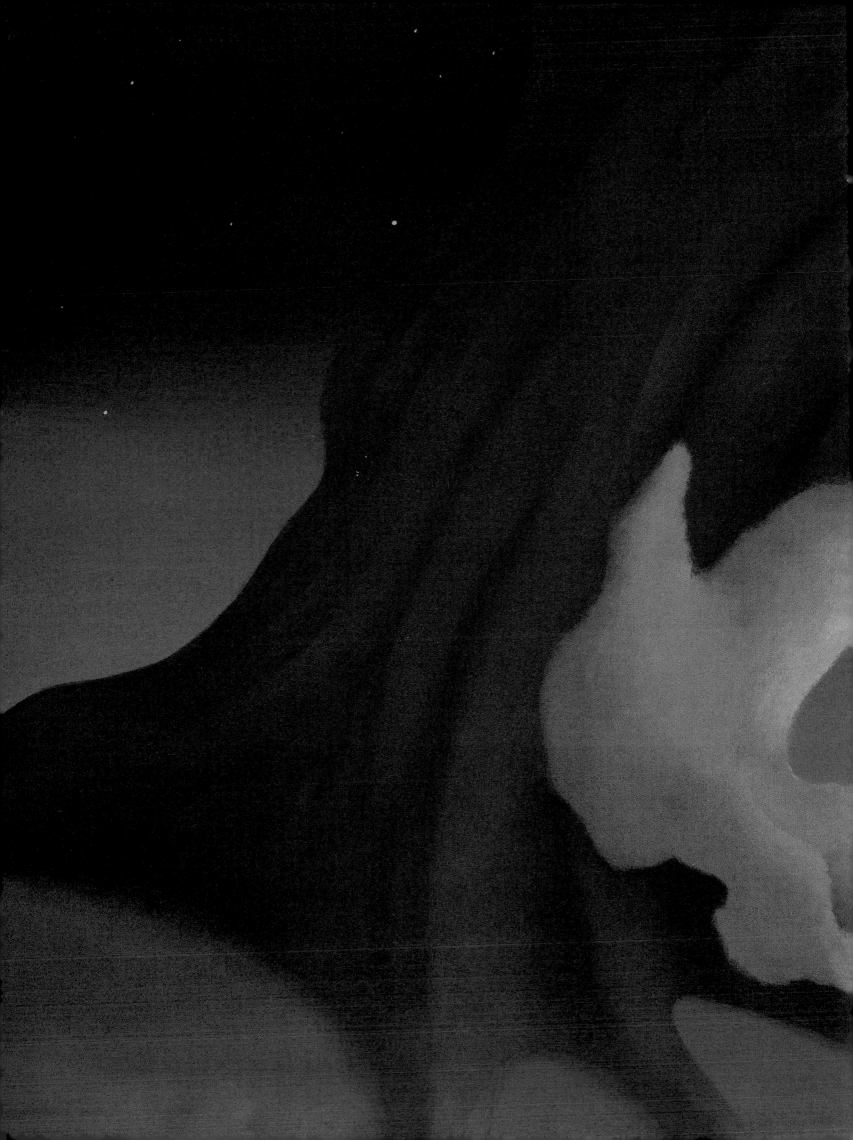

One very dark night, Alexander found himself in the
middle of nowhere.
He lay down by a tree and closed his eyes . . .
He could hear all sorts of noises coming from the countryside.
Were there wolves around here?
Were the snakes out tonight?

Suddenly, the clouds disappeared, revealing a sky
peppered with stars. Alexander began to count them,
remembering what Grandpa would say,
"If one is missing, there will always be another to replace it."

Comforted by this idea,
he fell asleep with a peaceful smile.

At dawn, Alexander was woken up by a new sound.
It was a tick . . . followed by a tock . . . tick . . . tock . . . . .
"It sounds like a clock," he thought, surprised.
"Who listens to a ticking clock this early in the morning?"
"No one, except . . . Grandpa!"

Alexander leaped with joy!

When Paradiso arrived,
The little boy asked him,
"The Land of Happiness, is it where I live?"
The bird did not reply . . .
Overjoyed, Alexander scribbled one last
postcard, placed it on the doormat,
and hid in the pumpkin field outside
his house.

With sleepy, half-closed eyes, Grandpa opened
the door. He saw the card, picked it up, and read it.
And then he smiled a very, very big smile! His eyes
sparkled like stars and his cheeks turned ruby red.

"Dear Grandpa,
This time, I've understood. I have found lots of
happiness everywhere, but the greatest happiness
is here with you!
Lots of love,
Alexander."

Alexander came out from behind the pumpkins, and Grandpa hugged him very, very tightly.
With Alexander in his arms, Grandpa asked,
"What if you and I went off together to find new lands of happiness?"
"Aren't you afraid your feet will hurt?" Alexander asked with surprise. "Or you'll catch a cold? Or we'll get lost?"

"With you," Grandpa replied, "never!"

Alexander and Grandpa set off on their journey
that very morning.
And Paradiso followed them up the mountains,
through the valleys, and into the skies,
because . . .

The Land of Happiness is everywhere where people are happy.